A catalogue record for this book is available from the British Library.

First edition

Published by Ladybird Books Ltd Loughborough Leicestershire UK

Printed in EC

Disney

The Jungle Book

Ladybird Books

Many strange legends are told of the jungles of India. One such tale is of Mowgli, a Man-cub who grew up in the jungle.

The story begins on a day long ago, when Bagheera the panther heard a strange sound coming from a little broken boat that had washed up on the river's edge. It was the sound of a baby crying. Bagheera looked in the boat and saw a Man-cub lying in a basket.

Had Bagheera known how his life would be changed by that Man-cub, he might have left the basket where it was. But he didn't. He picked it up and took it away with him.

Now that he had the Man-cub, Bagheera wasn't sure what to do with it, especially since the baby would soon need feeding.

Then the panther remembered a family of wolves that had recently been blessed with a litter of cubs. He left the Man-cub at the entrance to the wolves' den and let them do the rest.

A little wolf cub was the first to discover the basket. He sniffed it and said, "What kind of cub is this?"

Then the mother wolf approached the basket. Realising at once that this was a baby who needed looking after, she smiled. Mowgli stopped crying and smiled, too.

And that is how Mowgli found a family.

The seasons came and went, and Bagheera often visited the wolf den to see how the Man-cub was getting on. Mowgli and the wolf cubs were growing up together, playing happily with each other as any children would.

Bagheera was pleased that the Man-cub was so contented and well cared for. But he knew that one day Mowgli would have to go back to his own kind.

But one day, ten years after Bagheera had first found Mowgli, Shere Khan returned to the jungle.

Shere Khan was a fierce and ruthless tiger, who was greatly feared by all the animals. When he heard about Mowgli, Shere Khan decided to track him down and kill him. "The Man-cub may be harmless now," thought the tiger, "but soon he will be fully grown – and dangerous."

When the wolves heard that Shere Khan was looking for Mowgli, the elders called a meeting at Council Rock. Akela, the leader, spoke first.

"Shere Khan will surely kill the boy and all who try to protect him," Akela said. "He can no longer stay with the pack."

Rama, Mowgli's wolf-father, was upset. "The boy cannot survive in the jungle alone," he said. "There must be some way we can help him."

Bagheera, who had been watching from the branch of a tree, knew that Rama was right. He jumped down into the centre of the gathering. "Perhaps I can assist you," he announced. "I know a Man-village where the boy will be safe. I can take him there myself."

Reluctantly, Rama agreed that it would be best for Mowgli to return to the world of men. It was decided that Bagheera should take him at once.

And so, later that evening, Mowgli and Bagheera set out across the jungle.

Mowgli was feeling very cross. "I don't want to leave," he sulked. "I'm not afraid of Shere Khan, you know."

"Maybe not," replied Bagheera, "but you should be. Shere Khan is a dangerous enemy."

It was very late when
Bagheera stopped at the foot of
a big tree. "You'll be safer up
here," he said, helping Mowgli
to climb onto a high branch.

Mowgli was very tired and
didn't argue. He snuggled up
against Bagheera, and they
both fell fast asleep.

13

But they were not alone. Kaa the snake was hiding in the same tree.

"It's a Man-cub," hissed Kaa, winding his way down through the branches. "Yes, a delicious Man-cub!"

Mowgli, suddenly awake, found himself looking into Kaa's eyes. The snake swayed before him, making him dizzy.

"Go away!" shouted Mowgli. But he couldn't stop staring into Kaa's bright, piercing yellow eyes. Before he knew what had happened, Mowgli was in a trance.

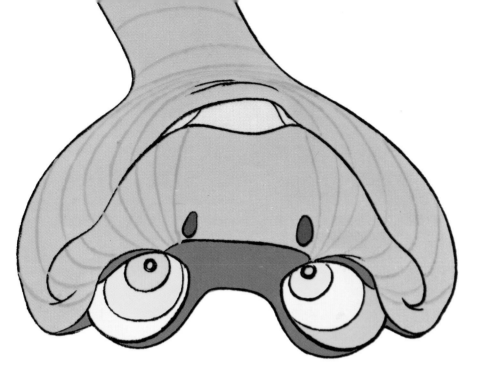

Kaa wrapped his long tail round Mowgli and began squeezing him tightly. Mowgli, helpless under Kaa's spell, couldn't move a muscle.

"Now I have you! What a tasty supper," said Kaa, opening his mouth wide.

Luckily, the snake's voice woke Bagheera, who saw instantly what was happening. He aimed a powerful blow right at the snake's jaw. *Whack!* The stunned snake fell to the ground with a thud. He slithered away, muttering angrily to himself.

Bagheera turned to Mowgli. "Tonight it was Kaa who tried to get you. Tomorrow it might be Shere Khan. Do you understand now why you must go to the Man-village? You aren't safe in the jungle on your own."

Mowgli said nothing. As far as he was concerned, the jungle was his home, and he always felt safe there.

Next morning, Mowgli and Bagheera were awakened by a terrible thundering, crashing noise.

"Hup, two, three, four!" a deep voice bellowed. "Keep it up, two, three, four!" Trees and branches rumbled, and the jungle shook.

"Oh, no," groaned Bagheera. "It's the dawn patrol."

Mowgli grabbed a vine and swung down to the ground to watch as a huge herd of elephants marched by. Leading the way was Colonel Hathi, a big bull elephant. As he shouted orders, the tired-looking troops followed in a line, trumpeting a military march.

Mowgli decided to follow the herd. He tried his best to march, stop, turn and change direction, all at Colonel Hathi's command. But he quickly became confused. All at once he found himself face to face with a baby elephant.

"Go the other way. Turn around," whispered Mowgli's new friend.

They turned and marched, and marched and turned. Mowgli was having a wonderful time.

"Living with an elephant herd would be a lot better than going to a Man-village," he decided.

Then, just when Mowgli thought he had got the knack of
military marching, Colonel Hathi bellowed, "Company,
HALT!"

The elephants came to a sudden stop, all piling on top of
one another.

"March, march, march. My feet are killing me," said an elephant called Winifred. "I'm going to request a transfer!"

"Silence in the ranks!" shouted Colonel Hathi.

"What kind of soldiers are you?" thundered Colonel Hathi, when he had the herd's attention. "Straighten up that line! Get ready for inspection!"

"What's inspection?" Mowgli asked his friend.

"You'll see," said the baby elephant.

Mowgli watched as all the elephants stood to attention and stuck their trunks in the air.

"Let's have a little more spit and polish on those bayonets," said Colonel Hathi, tapping an old elephant on the tusks.

"Yes, sir," the elephant replied.

"You'd better stick your trunk up in the air, too," the baby elephant said to Mowgli.

Mowgli stood straight and tall, and held his nose as high as he could.

Colonel Hathi smiled as he came to the baby elephant. "Let's keep those heels together, shall we, son?" he said.

"Okay, Pop... er, sir," the baby elephant replied.

"Well," snorted the colonel, as he came to Mowgli at last, "what have we here – a new recruit?" He grasped Mowgli in his trunk and held him up in order to get a better look at him.

"Why, it's a Man-cub!" he gasped. "This is treason! I'll have no Man-cub in *my* jungle!"

"It's not *your* jungle," said Mowgli defiantly.

Bagheera, who had been quietly following Mowgli at a distance, saw that it was time for him to step in.

"I can explain, Colonel Hathi," he said. "The Man-cub is with me. I'm taking him back to the Man-village."

"To stay?" asked the colonel.

"Yes," said Bagheera. "You have my word."

"Good," said Colonel Hathi. "But remember – an elephant never forgets!" With that, the colonel and his troops marched off, and Mowgli and Bagheera were on their way again.

"You were lucky I arrived when I did," said Bagheera to Mowgli. "Now, let's go before something else happens!"

"No," said Mowgli. "I don't want to leave the jungle, and I don't want to go to the Man-village. I can take care of myself – I know I can!"

Bagheera was getting tired of arguing with Mowgli. "You're going to the Man-village if I have to drag you every step of the way!"

Mowgli grabbed a tree trunk and stubbornly refused to let go. As Bagheera struggled to pull Mowgli away he lost his grip and fell tumbling into a river.

"That does it!" fumed Bagheera. "I've had enough. You're on your own!" And he stalked off.

Bagheera hadn't been gone long when Mowgli heard
singing, and a big, happy bear came shambling by.

"Hi there, Little Britches," said the bear. "I'm Baloo. Who
are you?"

Mowgli told the bear who he was and why he was alone.
When he finished his story, Baloo said, "Don't worry, kid. I'll
teach you how to survive in the jungle. Now, the first thing
I'm going to show you is how to growl like a bear. Come on,
scare me – like this."

Mowgli and Baloo soon became good friends. Baloo
showed Mowgli how to fight like a bear, and he gave him
rides on his back. Mowgli tickled Baloo until the bear's
stomach ached with laughter.

"I like being with you, Baloo," said Mowgli. "You're much
more fun than Bagheera!"

It wasn't long before Mowgli was hungry.

"There's lots to eat in the jungle," Baloo told him. "You
just have to know where to find it."

Baloo showed Mowgli how to pick fruit from a prickly plant without getting hurt. Mowgli was delighted to find that the fruit tasted delicious.

Then Baloo showed Mowgli how to get honey from the bees and bananas from the trees.

"Life in the jungle is easy," he told Mowgli, "once you know how to find the bare necessities!"

After their meal, Baloo and Mowgli sang and danced through the jungle.

The two friends sat down together to catch their breath. After a few minutes, Baloo said, "How about a boxing match?"

"Great!" said Mowgli, and he punched Baloo as hard as he could.

"Ow!" cried Baloo, pretending to be hurt. "You win!"

"See?" said Mowgli proudly. "I *can* take care of myself!"

"Of course you can, Little Britches," said Baloo. "And you're going to make a great bear!" He hoisted Mowgli onto his shoulders, and they started down the path together.

Suddenly Bagheera leapt down from a tree and stood in front of them.

"Just a minute!" he said to Baloo. "You're not going anywhere with that Man-cub. I knew I shouldn't have left him alone! He's coming to the Man-village with me."

"You can't take him there," protested Baloo. "Why, they'll... they'll make a Man out of him!"

"That's right," said Mowgli. "I'm staying here and learning to be a bear like Baloo!"

"No, you're not," insisted Bagheera. He leapt up onto a branch so he could look Baloo in the eye. "Shere Khan is near by, and he's looking for the Man-cub. Mowgli must come with me."

Baloo gave Bagheera's tail a sharp tug. "He's coming with *me*," he declared.

Bagheera was fed up. "Oh, very well," he said. "I just hope your luck holds out!" he called, as Baloo and Mowgli continued down the path.

When they got to the river, Baloo jumped in and floated along on his back. Mowgli rode on the bear's chest.

"I like being a bear," Mowgli told Baloo.

"And you're doing really well, Little Britches," said Baloo. "I told you it would be fun! Now, let's see if you can sing like a bear."

Baloo closed his eyes and began to sing. He didn't notice the monkeys looking down from the trees along the river bank.

When Baloo finished his song and opened his eyes, he was startled to see a monkey sitting on his chest where Mowgli had been. When he looked up, he saw that the monkeys had taken Mowgli and were holding him by the feet.

"Let go of me!" Mowgli was shouting.

"Hey, you," shouted Baloo, standing up in the water. "Take your flea-pickin' hands off my cub!"

The monkeys lowered Mowgli and swung him just out of
Baloo's reach. "Come and get him," they laughed tauntingly.
Baloo tried to grab Mowgli, but the monkeys were too fast for
him.

"Give me back my Man-cub!" Baloo shouted, shaking his
fist at them. The monkeys just kept laughing as they
disappeared into the trees with their captive.

Baloo scrambled out of the water and raced after the monkeys. He could see them passing Mowgli back and forth between them like a ball. But all he could do was shout at them and watch helplessly. There was no way he could stop them.

The monkeys were delighted. They began pelting Baloo with fruit, and two of them scampered down and managed to trip the big bear with a vine. As Baloo fell with a thud, the monkeys ran off, still holding on to Mowgli.

Baloo was still dazed from his fall when Bagheera caught up with him.

"Where's Mowgli?" Bagheera asked sternly. "What's happened to him?"

"The monkeys ambushed me," Baloo replied. "Thousands of 'em... "

"Monkeys?" said Bagheera. "They've probably taken him to that king of theirs in the ruins of the ancient temple. I hate to think what could happen to him there. Come on, we'd better get to the ruins before it's too late!"

For once, Baloo didn't argue with Bagheera. The two set off immediately.

Bagheera was right – the monkeys had taken Mowgli to their leader, King Louie.

"So," said King Louie, "you're the Man-cub. Tell me the secret of Man's fire, and you can stay in the jungle."

Mowgli said he didn't know how to make fire, but King Louie didn't believe him. He grabbed Mowgli's arm and hurled him towards the other monkeys. The monkeys swung Mowgli round and round, until he began to feel quite dizzy.

While the monkeys were dancing, Bagheera was watching from a hiding place in the ruins, waiting for the right moment to jump out and snatch Mowgli away.

All at once a big ape in a grass skirt danced in and joined the monkeys. No one but Mowgli and Bagheera realised that it was Baloo in disguise.

As Baloo danced, all the monkeys began to follow him, clapping their hands. King Louie, clapping faster than everyone else, was having a wonderful time.

Suddenly Baloo's coconut snout fell off, and the monkeys recognised him. "It's Baloo, the bear!" they all shouted, as Mowgli ran towards his friend.

51

Baloo grabbed Mowgli's arm and started to run, but King Louie grabbed Mowgli's other arm. As they pulled Mowgli back and forth, King Louie braced himself against one of the ancient columns.

All at once, the column began to crumble. Then, with a terrible creaking noise, the whole temple began to collapse!

Letting go of Mowgli, King Louie did his best to hold up the roof of the falling temple. Baloo let go of Mowgli, too, as he tried to hold up the other end of the roof.

Suddenly a fiendish look crossed Baloo's face. He had a wonderful idea!

Dropping his side of the
temple, Baloo rushed over and
began tickling King Louie. As
King Louie's shoulders shook
with laughter, he let go of the
temple roof.

Baloo ducked out just in
time, as the temple collapsed
into a pile of rubble.

Baloo joined Mowgli and Bagheera as they escaped.
Looking back one last time, they saw King Louie
standing amidst the debris, shaking his fist at them.

As soon as they found a safe place to spend the night, Mowgli fell asleep. Baloo sat at the water's edge admiring his black eye in the reflection below. Bagheera took the opportunity to talk to Baloo, and finally convinced him that it was far too dangerous for Mowgli to remain in the jungle. "It's up to you now," Bagheera told Baloo. "He won't listen to me."

But the next morning, when Baloo took Mowgli aside and tried to explain it all to him, Mowgli was furious. "You're just like Bagheera!" he shouted. "I won't go to the Man-village with you, either!" And he ran off into the jungle.

He ran a long way before he felt sure that Baloo and Bagheera weren't behind him. Finally, exhausted, Mowgli flopped down beneath a tree.

The next thing he knew, he was face to face with Kaa the python. "So nice to see you again," hissed Kaa, hoisting Mowgli up into the branch of a tree.

"Leave me alone," snapped Mowgli, pushing the snake's face away. "I'm not going to look at you. I know what you're trying to do."

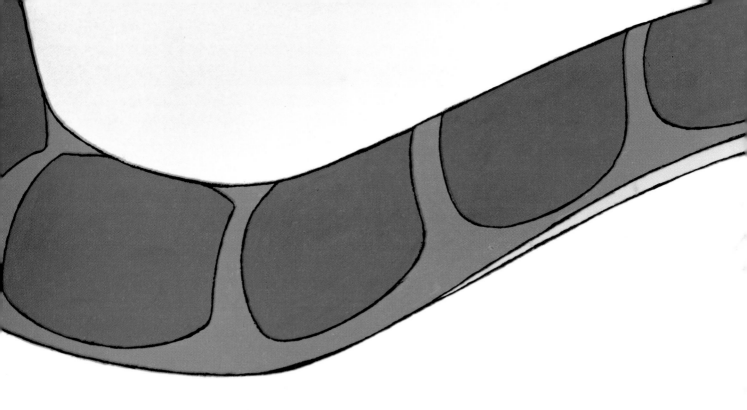

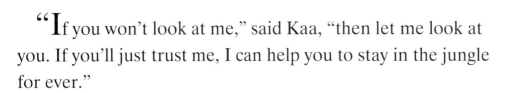

"If you won't look at me," said Kaa, "then let me look at you. If you'll just trust me, I can help you to stay in the jungle for ever."

"You can?" asked Mowgli.

"Certainly," replied Kaa. "Now, just shut your eyes..."

Mowgli's eyelids began to feel heavy, and soon they were closing. As Mowgli fell into a deep sleep, Kaa began to coil his body round the boy.

Suddenly Shere Khan, the great tiger, grabbed Kaa by the neck and pulled his head to the ground.

"Shere Khan! What a surprise!" gasped the snake.

"Who were you talking to up there?" asked Shere Khan, holding Kaa's head down.

"Talking? Er... I was talking to myself," replied Kaa. "I was just curling up for my nap... "

"You were talking to someone," said Shere Khan, as he scratched Kaa's nose with one of his huge claws. "Why don't you just show me who you've got hidden in your coils up there?"

"You know I would never hide anything from you, Shere Khan," said Kaa. All the while, he was slowly and carefully uncoiling his body, hoping he wouldn't disturb Mowgli.

At last Shere Khan seemed convinced that there was no one in the tree, and he stalked away, leaving a very frightened Kaa behind. Kaa was so shaken that he didn't even try to stop Mowgli when the boy awoke and slid down a vine to escape.

Mowgli ran as fast and as far as he could. Finally, he stopped by a pool to rest. He felt lonely and frightened, and he was beginning to wonder if Bagheera had been right all along.

A flock of vultures came by for a drink. They had never seen a Man-cub before, but they could see that Mowgli was unhappy. "Poor little guy," said a vulture called Buzzie. "You look like you haven't got a friend in the world."

"We'll be your friends!" said a vulture called Ziggy, putting a wing round Mowgli's shoulders.

All at once a sinister voice echoed through the jungle. "Thank you for detaining my victim."

The vultures whirled round. There, just a few feet away, sat Shere Khan.

The tiger stalked towards Mowgli, his yellow eyes unblinking.

The vultures all flapped away in fear. "Run! Run!" they screeched to Mowgli.

Then the jungle was very quiet, and Mowgli was face to face with his enemy.

Mowgli was terrified, but he tried hard not to show his fear. Summoning all his courage, he looked straight at Shere Khan and said, "I'm not scared of you!"

"But you must be," said the tiger. "Everyone in the jungle runs from Shere Khan."

"Well, I won't," declared Mowgli.

"I admire your spirit," said Shere Khan, "so I'll give you a sporting chance. I'll close my eyes and count to ten while you try to get away. Ready? One, two, three, four... "

The vultures, still circling above, again told Mowgli to run.

But Mowgli knew that Shere Khan could run faster. If he tried to run away, the tiger would surely catch him.

Instead, Mowgli chose to fight. He knew he didn't stand much of a chance against the huge tiger, but he grabbed a heavy stick and swung it at Shere Khan.

Furious that a tiny Man-cub had dared to attack him, Shere Khan gave a fierce roar and bared his claws, ready to lunge at Mowgli.

Then, just as Shere Khan pounced, Baloo suddenly jumped out of the bushes. "Run, Mowgli! Run!" he shouted, as he tried to stop the tiger.

But Shere Khan was not to be stopped. "Out of my way, you big oaf," he snarled, tearing past Baloo.

Mowgli ran. He ran as fast as he could. But Shere Khan was so close behind him that he could feel the tiger's hot breath on his neck.

Baloo did the only thing he could – he grabbed the tiger by the tail. And the plan worked. It slowed down Shere Khan just enough to stop him catching Mowgli.

The vultures flew down to Mowgli's rescue and carried him off to safety.

"You can let go now, Baloo," Buzzie called.

"Are you kidding?" replied Baloo. "There's teeth on the other end!"

Suddenly Shere Khan spun round and, with one powerful blow, knocked Baloo over backwards. Just as the bear landed with a thud, a flash of lightning lit up the jungle. Thunder boomed, and another streak of lightning crashed into a nearby tree, setting it ablaze. Shere Khan drew back in terror and let out a roar.

"Fire!" squawked Buzzie. "That's the only thing old Stripes is afraid of! You get the fire, Mowgli. We'll help you do the rest!"

The vultures carried Mowgli to the tree and held him low enough to grab a burning branch. Then they set him lightly on the ground.

Mowgli now had a weapon that could save Baloo's life. Holding the burning branch, he started towards Shere Khan, who was about to sink his mighty claws into the helpless bear.

Shere Khan turned to watch Mowgli approach. "This time, Man-cub, you won't escape," he growled, padding towards him.

The tiger didn't get far. From high above, the vultures swooped down on him, pecking at his head and pulling his whiskers.

"Stay out of this, you mangy fools!" roared Shere Khan. "I'll tear you to pieces!"

While the enraged tiger clawed furiously at the vultures, Mowgli was able to sneak up behind him and tie the blazing branch to his tail.

"Look behind you, chum!" called the vultures. Shere Khan looked – and his terrified scream could be heard for miles. Desperately, he sped away, trying to escape the fiery branch.

"That's the last we'll see of him!" croaked Buzzie triumphantly.

Bagheera had finally caught up with Mowgli, and together they tried to rouse Baloo.

"Baloo, please get up," pleaded Mowgli. But Baloo remained motionless. "What's wrong with him?" said Mowgli, beginning to cry. "Why won't he wake up?"

"You've got to be brave, Mowgli," said Bagheera, gently. "Baloo has laid down his life for you. Come, it's best we leave now." He turned and walked slowly away.

"Don't stop, Baggy!" exclaimed Baloo, sitting up. "You're doing great."

"Why, you big fraud!" sputtered Bagheera.

Mowgli threw his arms round Baloo's neck. "Good old Papa Bear!" he laughed.

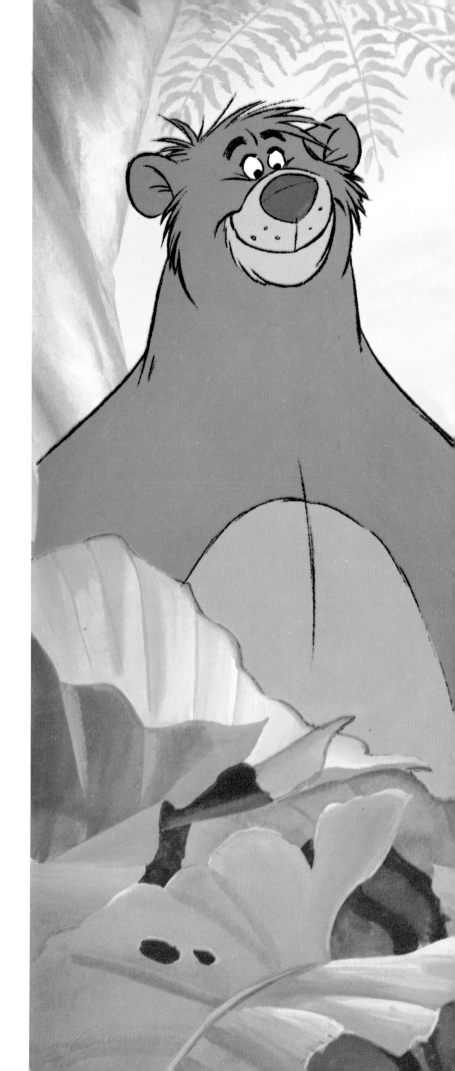

Next morning, the three friends went down to the river for a drink. As they drew near, they heard singing.

"What's that?" asked Mowgli. "I've never heard anything like that before."

"Oh, never mind that," said Baloo, trying to get a little boxing match going with Mowgli. But Mowgli wasn't paying attention to him.

Mowgli crept closer to the singing. As he parted the branches, he saw a young girl coming down to the river to get some water. Behind her was a little cluster of houses.

"Bagheera, what's that?" asked Mowgli.

"It's the Man-village," Bagheera replied.

"No," said Mowgli. "I mean *that.*" He pointed to the girl. "I've never seen one before."

"Go on, Mowgli," said Bagheera. "Go and have a closer look."

As the girl knelt by the river's edge, Mowgli climbed into a tree to watch her. He was enthralled.

The girl leaned over and saw Mowgli's reflection in the water. Just at that moment, the branch broke and Mowgli fell into the water beside her.

The girl giggled and smiled at him. Mowgli, entranced, helped her to lift the water jug out of the river and onto her head. He followed her to the village. Every now and then, she looked back over her shoulder and smiled at him.

"It was bound to happen," said Bagheera, as he and Baloo watched Mowgli walk into the village. "He's where he belongs now."

"I guess you're right," Baloo sighed. "But I still think he would have made one swell bear."

Together, the two friends went back to the jungle where they belonged, pleased that their beloved Man-cub would now grow up happily and safely.